KU-474-649

To **ADAM**

Love from
....

"What's that horrid stuff?" asks Adam,
pointing at the telly.
"That's plastic rubbish," Mum explains.
"It's horrible and smelly."

So why's it floating everywhere?
How come it's in the sea?
Why are the turtles getting stuck?
They should be **swimming free**!

When plastic was invented,
everybody was amazed.
"What is this awesome stuff?" they said.
It took hold like a craze.

But now we know that plastic's not
the wonder we all thought.
It's **poisoning our planet**, Adam;
this message must be taught.

So c'mon, Adam, the time is now,
to wage a **war on waste**.
Put on that suit and grab your mask,
we really must make haste.

The oceans can do many things,
but they can't clean up this mess.
It's up to us to fix it, Adam.
There are things we must address....

Don't let go of that balloon – it ends up in the sea!

The plastic thrown away each year
could circle the earth **FOUR** times.

Every minute, one rubbish truck of plastic is d u m p e d into our oceans.

Almost **half** of the rubbish in the oceans is left behind by fishermen.

An octopus cries, "Adam, help!
My legs are stuck in cups.
The oceans contain tonnes of these.
We need to clean them up!"

"When we buy drinks that look like this,
the cups and lids get thrown."
Adam says, "I know the answer.
I'll tell people: **'BRING YOUR OWN!'**"

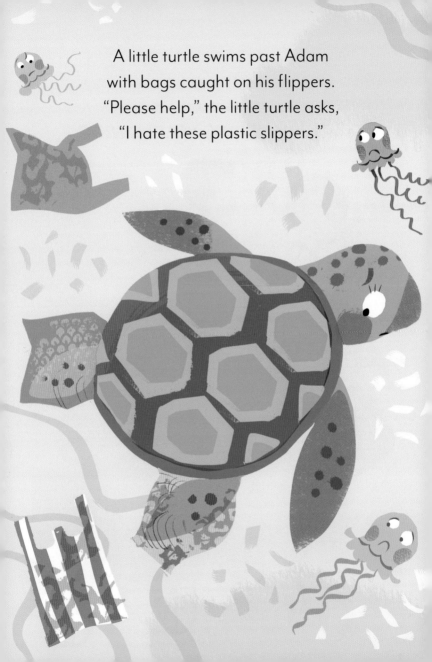

A little turtle swims past Adam
with bags caught on his flippers.
"Please help," the little turtle asks,
"I hate these plastic slippers."

"Fruit and veg in plastic bags?
Let's stop this single-use."
Adam says, "I've got it.
Tell everyone to **'BUY THEM LOOSE!'**"

Adam swims up to see the shore.
"Hi, Crab. What's in your claws?"
The crab frowns back, "I'm cleaning up
this mess of plastic straws."

"The beach is where we live and play.
It's where we go to bed."
Adam says, "We'll help out by using
PAPER STRAWS instead."

This dolphin's caught up in a net
and cannot swim about.
Adam dives back in to save her.
"You poor thing; I'll get you out!"

Adam asks her, "What can we all do?
This really needs to stop."
She says, "Tell your fishermen to
PICK UP EVERYTHING they drop."

Adam's helped clear up the nets,
the straws, the nasty foam.

Adam's changing how he acts
to make the oceans better.
He even asks Mum, **"Who's in charge?"**
so he can write a letter.

Adam says, "We must take action.
There's really no excuse.
To save our underwater friends
we must **reduce our use**!"

Adam is telling his whole class,
"Change can start with you!"

ADAM
IS MY
HERO

"Try trading old toys with your mates. **DON'T ALWAYS BUY** things new!"

"I'm Adam, Guardian of the Seas,
and I will show the way.
I'll fight to **save the oceans** for us,
every single day!"

ADAM SAVES THE OCEANS

Adam! Become a Plastic Hero!

Tick everything you will (or already!) do to take action against plastic pollution.

Use paper straws (or get a cool reusable straw!) ☐

Don't flush wet wipes down the toilet ☐

Swap toys with my friends instead of asking for new ones ☐

Talk to my family about using less plastic ☐

Carry my food in a lunch box ☐

Make my own snacks ☐

Recycle as much plastic as possible ☐

Tell my friends what I've learned ☐

No littering ☐

Ask everyone to stop using glitter and sequins ☐

Get a reusable water bottle ☐

Hey Adam, if you can stop using single-use plastic you will make a **BIG** difference!

Adam, write four things you will tell your friends and family about plastic.

Adam's Plastic Pledge

I, Adam, promise to reduce my plastic use to help save my fishy friends.

Sign here: _____

Date: _____

Written by J.D. Green
Illustrated by Ela Smietanka
Designed by Nicky Scott

First published by HOMETOWN WORLD in 2019
Hometown World Ltd
1 Queen Street
Bath
BA1 1HE

Visit
www.hometownworld.co.uk

Follow us @hometownworldbooks

MIX
Paper from
responsible sources
FSC® C023419

Hometown World